I0578925

NOT OF THIS WORLD

JEFF COLEMAN

Published internationally by Pallid Visions®
PO Box 5943, Buena Park, CA 90622, United States.

Cover art and design ©2020 Alejandro Comesaña.

This book is a work of fiction. Any similarity between the characters and situations within its pages and places or persons, living or dead, is unintentional and coincidental.

For more information about the author, visit his homepage:
https://blog.jeffcolemanwrites.com/

ISBN 978-1-945997-20-4 (E-book)
ISBN 978-1-945997-19-8 (Hardcover)
ISBN 978-1-945997-18-1 (Paperback)

Library of Congress Control Number: 2020921824
First Edition.

Contents

Acknowledgments vii

Chapter 1. 1

Chapter 2. 7

Chapter 3. 11

Chapter 4. 15

Chapter 5. 19

Chapter 6. 25

Chapter 7. 29

Chapter 8. 33

Chapter 9. 37

Chapter 10. 43

Chapter 11. 49

Chapter 12. 53

Chapter 13. 55

Chapter 14. 57

Chapter 15. 61

Chapter 16. 65

Chapter 17. 69

Chapter 18. 73

Chapter 19. 77

Chapter 20. 83

Chapter 21. 87

Acknowledgments

This book is dedicated, first and foremost, to my wife and parents. You guys have helped me out in so many different ways. What else is there to say but "thank you!"

As always, I have to give a special shout out to my patrons. You guys have been a source of constant encourgement and support and I'll be forever in your debt. If you became a patron after November 4, 2020, I'm sorry I wasn't able to list you here. But know that you, too, hold a special place in my heart, and that this book wouldn't have been possible without you.

Melissa Iwata

"JonBoy" Maddron

Monica A. Franklin

Anthony Colannino

Voni Colannino

Rae Taylor

Lisa Plante

Jeannine Cook-Battles

Laura Anne StJohn

Lisa Castel

Alixevette Solstice

Jessica Parkko

B.K.

Pat Williamson

Karen Palumar

Tonya Fasciglione

Dyan Lease

Angela Escarcega

Quiarrah

Julia Davis

Anna Garcia-Centner

Karen Sutton

James Mazur Jr.

1.

LIKE AN EXPLORER, Diane set off across the abstract landscapes of Excel in search of answers that only the numbers on her spreadsheet could provide. Like sages, they whispered their arcane secrets, and Diane, with ear inclined, did her best to listen.

But instead of answers she heard cries. Startled, Diane lost focus. The numbers scattered, and whatever they'd been about to tell her sank into the depths and was lost.

Annoyed, she hunched closer to her laptop until the screen filled most of her vision. She spent a few more minutes copy-pasting data into her spreadsheet, then sighed, stood up from her desk, and walked toward the window. She opened the blinds and squinted, stunned by the sudden burst of light.

The cries were those of children. There was a park by her office, and every day after lunch the nearby elementary school would escort their summer session students, along with a group of volunteer parents, for their afternoon recess.

The eighth-story window afforded her a perfect view of the park below, and she watched the children run around the playground like a swarm of locusts. There was a time when Diane would have also enjoyed gliding on the swings or tumbling down the slide. But then she'd removed her childhood like a worn-out cloak and donned the prim, sophisticated attire of adulthood.

Spotting a mother attending to a crying girl, a sharp pang of jealousy stabbed her in the side. She staggered back a little, surprised by the visceral force of the emotion, and looked away.

Her eyes drifted to the tree.

It had been catching her attention since she'd started with the company a year and a half ago. Diane didn't like the uncomfortable questions that sprang to mind whenever she looked at it—*What's my purpose in the world? Where do I belong?*—and she always tried to ignore it. Nevertheless, it was difficult to look away.

Now her eyes fell upon its weathered branches, seeming to tower over her even from her eighth-story vantage point. She thought she could hear it calling, reaching out to her in a language without words—a soft primordial whisper, hardly there at all. If only she could strain her ears enough to hear…

But that was only her imagination, and Diane chided herself for entertaining the thought. She wasn't a kid anymore. It was good old-fashioned education and hard work that had gotten her to where she was today, not childish notions like sentient trees.

It's just a tree. Grow up, Diane.

But it wasn't just a tree, and somewhere in the dungeon of her heart, where her younger self was serving a life sentence, there lived a primal knowledge of the tree's power, however much her adult self tried to deny it.

"Diane?"

She jumped and turned. There in the doorway stood Ronald, the CEO, donning some variation of the same gray suit he wore every day to the office.

"Sorry," he said, holding up his hands. "I didn't mean to startle you."

"It's fine," she said, and just like that, the real world came rushing back.

"Can I come in?"

"Of course." As Diane returned to her laptop on wobbly feet, she gestured for him to take a seat.

"Is this a bad time?"

She watched Ronald sit on the opposite side of her desk, and with a small shake of her head, she said, "No, I was just thinking. There's so much to get a handle on at once."

"I'm sure you'll figure it out. You've certainly done well so far. The company hasn't seen this kind of growth since it was founded."

Diane suppressed what would have been a wide and eager grin. Praise validated her self-worth, and sometimes, for a little while, at least, it helped her to forget the dark thoughts that swirled around inside her head whenever she spent too much time alone.

"Just doing my job."

Ronald waved the comment away. "Don't be modest, Diane. You're good and we're lucky to have you."

This time, she allowed herself a small smile.

"Do you think you'll be ready to present your plans for the company tomorrow? I'm eager to discuss your progress with the other officers."

Uneasy, Diane glanced at the half-baked numbers on her spreadsheet. She still had a lot left to do. She could present tomorrow if it was absolutely necessary, but it wouldn't give her much time to prepare.

"It's okay if you need more time," he clarified.

"No, of course I can." The answer was a knee-jerk reaction.

"Are you sure?"

"I just have to crunch a few more numbers." What she didn't tell him was that she also had to structure her notes, outline her speech, and prepare a ton of technical slides.

"Excellent." Ronald's jubilant expression triggered another rush of prideful pleasure. "We'll gather in the conference room for lunch. I can't wait to hear how you're going to move us forward." Ronald got up, shook her hand, and left.

Looking once more at the laptop, Diane began to speed through all the important points she wanted to cover. But as she toggled through her data, she thought she could feel the tree again.

It's speaking to me; I know it is.

She had no idea what it was trying to say, but it felt like some kind of summons, or perhaps an invitation. Suddenly the numbers on the screen seemed part of an entirely unfamiliar world, sterile, alien, and cold. Rattled, she struggled to decipher their meanings. But it was impossible to focus and by five-thirty, she decided she'd be better off finishing from home.

It was the first time in years that Diane had left the office on time.

2.

THE SUN HUNG LOW when Diane stepped outside. Anxious and uncertain, she peered at the horizon, beginning her daily trek through the park. With only a quarter of a mile between the office and her apartment, it was the surest route home. If she'd driven a car, it would have taken her longer just to deal with the traffic lights.

A breeze swept through the open field as Diane walked with her head down, and despite the summer heat, she crossed her arms over her breasts to fend off the cold. Focused once more on work, her mind delved into a roiling sea of variables and probabilities. Starting with where the company stood today, she ran through all the potential scenarios, making mental projections at one, three, six, and twelve months in the future. She would do the same tomorrow and the day after that. It was how she stayed at the top of her game, how she survived the rocks that life always pelted from a distance.

You have to be strong, Diane. Life isn't going to hand you gold on a silver platter. Her foster mother had told her that many times over the course of her childhood. She cast the thought aside. It didn't matter what the woman had said. They hadn't spoken in years.

PropelIt, a small digital advertising agency in Irvine, had brought her on board as a Business Strategies Analyst. The company had been surviving since its founding in the early 2000s but was stuck in a sort of half-life, never having profited enough to expand. Diane was there to help them grow. She'd already met with some success—so much, in fact, that they didn't have the infrastructure or the workforce in place to handle the extra volume of inquiries and sales. It would be rough sailing until the second phase of her plan was complete.

Speaking of rough sailing, why had she agreed to give her presentation on such short notice? Diane thought of all the things she had left to do and her heart raced.

He said it's okay if I need more time, so why didn't I tell him?

Because it was imperative for her to be ready at the drop of a hat. That was how she was able to play the part of the office hero, and by doing so, secure her place in the world.

How could she have gotten so little done today? She hadn't even started her slides. Instead the tree had distracted her.

Grow up, Diane.

She looked up then, as if the thought were a signal, and was startled to see that she was now standing beside the tree. A sprawling oak, gnarled and ancient, its branches loomed, vast serpentine tendrils reaching for the sky. There was a stirring in a part of herself she'd neglected for years, and it was only through an incredible force of will that she held the emotion at bay.

Diane listened to the leaves and the sound they made in the wind—a dry, murmuring whisper—and for a moment, she believed once more that the tree was trying to speak.

The light of the setting sun had burst through the tree's canopy, a bright empyrean gold that capped it like a celestial crown. She wanted to pull her eyes away, to continue walking, but she felt as though something had seized control of her limbs. The image branded itself in her mind, and she blinked once, twice, three times before the spell was broken and she was able to move on.

When, at last, Diane continued her walk home, she found that all thoughts of her presentation had fled, abandoning her to a moment of terrifying interior silence.

Even after clearing the park, she thought she could still hear the tree and its indecipherable whispers, and she berated herself for the fact that goosebumps now prickled over her arms and legs.

3.

GROW UP, DIANE.

It had been her foster mother's motto when Diane was young. It was what she would say whenever Diane got jealous because the woman was paying more attention to her biological children than to her.

The world doesn't revolve around you.

Her foster parents had given her everything she needed physically. They'd fed her. Clothed her. Taken her to the doctor when she was sick. They'd never abused her, a fate that befell so many other foster children, so what right did she have to complain?

Diane was discovered as a baby outside the Buena Park Library in a cardboard box, and nobody had ever found her true parents. Her origins were a mystery. She didn't even know her birthday.

As a child, she spent a lot of time in her room alone. It was easier that way, not having to watch her foster parents shower her brothers and sisters with the kind of love she knew they would never offer her. But Diane had never complained, because complaining was something little girls did, not big grown-up adults. Even now, whenever she caught herself crying, she'd mutter her foster mother's motto under her breath to steady herself.

Grow up, Diane.

She studied hard in high school and drove herself to exhaustion in an effort to graduate at the top of her class. Afterward she enrolled in a four-year university, where she received her degree in business administration, then worked her ass off in the private sector. Diane was determined to stand out, to prove she was better than everyone else, because she needed to know there was a place in the world where she could do well and, most importantly, a place in the world where she could *belong*.

But even though she tried so hard, there was always something missing, and it seemed that each success drove her further into isolation. She watched from a distance while her coworkers forged friendships and relationships, and like a zoologist studying a herd of some exotic species, she could never quite make sense of their interactions. Standing out, it seemed, was not enough. But Diane knew no other way, and with time, work became the drug she used to dull the edge of that bleak realization.

A campus Christian had approached her once on the way

to class and told her, "Our kingdom is not of this world." More and more, that was how she felt, like she was *not of this world*. It was the reason she never made friends, the reason she never fell in love. Diane told herself it was for the sake of her career, but deep down she knew that was bullshit. She was acquainted with plenty of career women like herself who managed to balance full-time jobs with healthy families and relationships. The truth was that somewhere deep inside, she knew she didn't belong and that she was forever destined to remain on the outside looking in.

Grow up, Diane.
Grow up.

4.

DIANE SAT ON THE COUCH in the darkness of her apartment, exhausted, her computer resting on her lap. What time was it? She moved her mouse to the bottom of the screen. 11:45 p.m. God. She reached up to rub her burning eyes and lay back, the cushion warm and inviting. But she couldn't sleep. Not yet. There was so much work left to do.

Just a few minutes.

The temptation to close her eyes and rest was difficult to ignore. All the energy was draining out of her, as if someone had administered a potent sedative. Her eyes began to droop.

Just a few minutes. So tired. A half hour, a quick power nap, and then—

DIANE IS RUNNING, and the rest of the world is changing around her. With every step, she sweeps across mountains and seas, deserts and plains. All the while, she can hear her mother—

her true mother—calling from a great distance while entire worlds streak by in an indeterminate blur.

The voice of her true mother is getting closer, and all Diane has to do is reach for it, let it embrace her, let it take her into its arms. Then everything will be all right.

Grow up, Diane.

The words crash down around her, a rumbling quake in the fabric of her reality. The space surrounding Diane quivers, wobbles, spins.

Grow up, Diane. Grow up!

The words disorient her, and she can no longer find her way. All around, the world begins to melt like candle wax.

Mom, she thinks. *I have to find Mom.* But every time she turns, there's that other voice, telling her to grow up, telling her she isn't a little girl anymore.

Grow up, Diane!

Grow up, Diane!

Grow—

DIANE'S EYES POPPED OPEN. Still seized by panic, it took her a few moments to remember she was in her apartment. By then the dream, though stark and vivid at the point of waking, had already started to recede, and she found herself struggling to piece it together.

Had it been about family? Running away and getting lost? She couldn't remember anymore, only that it had terrified her and left her with the lingering sense that she was not where she belonged.

I'm right here where I'm supposed to be. It was just a dream. Grow up, Diane.

She glanced down, where the computer now slept on her lap. Her presentation.

Shit!

Diane was exhausted, but she had to finish her work. The company was at a crucial juncture. She knew the CEO and other officers were on her side, that they were enthusiastic about what she had in store for the future of the company, but she couldn't take that for granted. She had to be at the top of her game.

Or what?

Or I'll lose my job, that's what.

Okay, maybe that was an overreaction. Still, better safe than sorry. Her work was all she had. If she failed, the fragile life she'd built around herself would come tumbling down, leaving only the frightened little girl she tried so hard to push away.

So Diane stayed up until 5:30 a.m., ignoring the soreness in her eyes and the headache jackhammering her skull. When she finally finished, she slept for an hour, got up, took an aspirin, and pushed herself out the door.

5.

DIANE SAT AT ONE END of a long black table, flanked on both sides by the company's officers with Ronald, the CEO, sitting across from her.

"Well," Ronald said when it appeared everyone had arrived, "I guess we should get started. Diane will present to us this afternoon. I'm excited to hear what she has to say. Her work so far has been impressive and I'm eager to learn what she has in store for us next. But I'll let her get to that. Diane?"

Sleep deprived and head pounding, Diane felt the clapping that followed like a dozen wrecking balls all smashing into her skull at once. But she soldiered on, forcing a smile as she rose from her seat. She stood before the room, took a deep breath, and began to speak.

"Thank you, Ronald. It's great to be here with all of you. We've had a strong fiscal year, with company growth exceeding our wildest expectations."

Smiles were shown. Heads were nodded.

Diane opened her laptop, which had already been connected to the projector, and after she loaded her presentation, the wall behind her exploded into a larger-than-life display of her last-minute work.

She grabbed her wireless pointer and backed away so she could be closer to the screen. "Today's presentation will be broken into three sections." She pointed to the first slide, an overview of what they would be hearing about for the next half hour. "First, I'll cover our current advertising campaigns. I'll talk about which platforms are performing and which ones aren't. Next, I'll go over our planned transition to an automated platform, including how we'll migrate existing clients and capture future leads. Finally, I'll close with my projections for the following year."

Click.

More smiles. More nods. This was going well.

"We'll also cover customer retention and its impact on future sales, but first—"

Then a voice, or something like a voice, crashed into Diane's head and forced everything else out. The sound was urgent, plaintive, and impossible to ignore. Something was trying to communicate with her, but she couldn't understand its language.

Grow up, Diane. You've got a presentation to finish.

"But first—" Diane repeated, shaking herself off. "First, I

want to compare the various platforms and their efficacy, make suggestions to further optimize our budget, and—"

There, again, that desperate alien voice, obliterating whatever Diane had been about to say next. A violent spasm caused her head to jerk back, as if her body were hell-bent on locating the source of that impossible sound with or without her cooperation.

What's happening?

All of this had to be her imagination, but she couldn't quite convince herself. Then it came to her in a flash of high-definition absurdity.

The tree. It was calling to her.

But that was ridiculous. Of all the things in the world that could have been trying to communicate with her, the tree was certainly the least likely. Trees were no more conscious than vegetables. And yet, as mad as the prospect was, her heart swelled with such strong certainty that she found herself questioning her sanity.

An image exploded in Diane's mind, vibrant and lucid. For a moment it was all she could see. There was the tree standing in the center of the park, its roots running deep beneath the earth, then beyond, down into the fabric of the cosmos. And behind it, the setting sun, framing the branches and leaves in heavenly tones of gold. Royalty. The tree was royalty. A mad thought, but true just the same.

Then the light in her head switched off and the vision disappeared, and when Diane regained awareness of her surroundings, she was standing before the company's officers, dazed and at a loss for words.

"Diane," Ronald asked, "are you okay?"

"I—" But she didn't have any idea how to respond, and it wasn't until the officers began moving toward her that her mind finally rebooted.

The presentation. She'd been in the middle of her presentation. And then… And then her imagination had hijacked the meeting and ruined everything.

Grow the fuck up, Diane!

Oh God, she'd made a complete ass of herself. How long had she been out? How long had she been standing there like a crazy woman, staring off into space?

Am I crazy?

The world wobbled, and Diane put a hand out to the table for support. She needed air. Her vision grew fuzzy and white around the edges and she began to feel lightheaded. She was just about to crumple like a rag doll when Amanda, the CFO, reached out to stop her fall.

"Diane, are you okay? Someone call an ambulance!"

"No, I—" But what could she say? A childish fantasy had derailed her very important grown-up presentation? "I think I need to lie down. I think—"

The voice in Diane's head picked up again, rising in volume and intensity until she felt like clapping her hands over her ears. She couldn't take this anymore. She had to get out. But her presentation— No, it was too late for that. The best she could hope for was some well-placed excuses that might give her the time she needed to regroup.

"I'm fine," Diane said, not liking the breathless quality of her voice. "Really. I think I just over extended myself. I was sick last night, I knew I probably shouldn't have come in, but the presentation, it was important, and I—"

She looked around the room, and for the first time she registered everyone's shocked expressions, including that of a thoroughly bewildered Ronald.

"—I wanted to try and get it done," she finished, then descended into an awkward, uncertain silence.

Amanda offered her hand but Diane refused it and stumbled backward toward the door.

"I'll be fine," she said, panicking. All the while she could hear the echo of that other voice, burned into her mind.

She turned down their repeated insistence that they call the paramedics and assured them she'd be fine, that she just needed rest. But she suspected from the way the officer's faces had transformed—the narrowed eyes, the compressed lips—that she'd lost at least half the room. She tried not to look into their eyes.

Until today, Diane's work had been her crowning achievement, the one thing she could be secure in above all else. Now, in the aftermath of her sudden mental breakdown, the office seemed hostile and unfamiliar, a place to which she could no longer relate, a place where she no longer *belonged*. She was a stranger here, an unwelcome foreigner whose visa had been unceremoniously revoked.

It was time for her to go. *Now*.

"I'm sorry," she said, not bothering to retrieve her laptop.

Just like that, before anyone could reply, she sailed through the door with her head down and exited the room.

6.

NOW DIANE PERCHED ON A BENCH in the middle of the park, staring at the tree with dark, bloodshot eyes. After her meltdown in the conference room, she'd left the building. She'd planned on returning home, but somehow she knew she'd end up here instead.

As she gazed at the tree—tall, ancient, transcendent—she imagined it gazed back at her, that it could read her mind as well as her soul. An attraction emanated from the tree's core like a gravitational field, and Diane could feel it pulling her in against her will. She'd tried to dig her heels in, had tried to keep herself anchored, but it was uprooting her, tearing her away from her center and from everything she'd ever known.

Grow up, Diane.

The automatic thought skimmed across the surface of her mind like a pebble across a lake, but she was no longer listening. Instead, she was hearing another voice, an otherworldly whisper that intertwined with the many complex silences in her heart.

The words remained indecipherable, but one thing was clear from its imperative tone: it was a summons, and Diane, to her horror, found herself rising from the bench to meet its call.

The tree, she thought groggily, was some kind of avatar, a symbol of a very different sort of life. She pressed her hands to the bark, taking in its rough and calloused form. Half asleep, eyes half closed, she pushed her fingers into the nooks and crevices, searching for the force that had been trying so hard to make contact.

Soon enough she found it: the lifeblood of the tree, a thrumming energy that churned through every inch of the trunk like a raging rapid. Touching it was like touching a live wire and, jolted, she shook with the earth-shattering force of its never-ending flow. That same energy now coursed through her, and it opened her eyes to another world.

This isn't where I belong.

She had no idea where the thought had come from, but she found herself longing for the tree or whatever entity it represented to wrap its arms around her and sweep her away to someplace other.

To my true home.

All Diane had ever wanted was to belong, and now, the tree was showing her the way forward to a place where she could finally fit in.

"Take me," she said, not realizing she was speaking out loud.

In that moment, she was prepared to go wherever the tree could take her.

Grow up, Diane!

This time, the automatic thought was a sucker punch to the stomach. It slammed down like an invisible stone wall and cut her off from the tree's power. All at once her hands turned hot, as if she'd placed them atop a burning stove, and she wrenched them away, throwing herself back into the grass.

For a moment she lay there, uncomprehending, numb, and motionless, with her eyes angled up toward the light spilling through the treetop. Then a blocked mental gear shifted, and the rational side of her brain kicked back into motion.

Eyes wide, Diane stumbled to her feet and backed away from the tree with broad, clumsy steps.

It's just a tree!

But it wasn't just a tree. It was so much more.

I'm crazy.

But she wasn't crazy either.

I can't leave this life. I have too many responsibilities.

And then she laughed a little, a quiet, half-mad titter.

I was talking to a fucking tree.

She stared up at it, towering over her like an Elder God, then turned and sprinted back to her apartment.

7.

THE DARKNESS OF SLEEP descends, and once more Diane finds herself running, the world shifting around her as she moves. She's been searching for hours, though she doesn't know what for. Alone and afraid, she traverses the sands of time, the cracks between the cosmos. She turns, and her surroundings resolve into the Buena Park Library, where once, long ago, she was abandoned. Diane looks down and sees a cardboard box lying beside the locked front door—*My cardboard box*, she thinks. Inside is an infant, bundled in woolen clothes.

That's me.

An irrational fear takes hold. She's going to be abandoned again. She's lived her entire life in isolation, and now things are coming full circle. She's going to be abandoned in this alien world and fostered by a woman who shows her the most minimal kind of love. Worst of all, she'll have to live with the knowledge that she wasn't wanted in the first place and that her true mother loved her even less.

Then a voice stirs in the back of her mind like a dusty, half-forgotten sigh. She's heard this voice before, she thinks, but this time it's louder, clearer. Even now, in this other world, the true meaning of the words eludes her. Nevertheless, a picture forms: a celestial cradle, rocking on the precipice between two worlds, and a woman who isn't a woman, crowned in starlight and radiating love like a star in miniature.

You are loved, that vision seemed to say. *You were never unwanted.*

"Mom?"

Diane moves toward her, but the vision fractures like stained glass, and when she looks again, the woman is gone.

"Mom, where are you?"

I have to find the tree, she thinks, though she can't say which tree or why the tree is so important.

Diane runs off in search of it and the world shifts around her.

Grow up, Diane.

The familiar thought bursts into her head unbidden and she stops, dumbstruck, paralyzed by fear. She tries to push it away, but it clangs over and over through her head like a struck gong, implacable, only rising in volume and intensity with each iteration.

Grow up, Diane.

Grow up, Diane.

Grow up, Diane.

She presses her hands against her ears to filter out the noise, but the sound is deafening and she can't make it go away. The warden of her childhood self is waking and it will not allow her to roam free much longer.

Grow up, Diane.

"No! Go away! I don't want to grow up!"

Grow up, Diane.

Again, she hears the voice, though it's more distant than before and seems to come to her from the other end of an impossibly long tunnel.

My mother. She's trying to speak.

"I'm coming," Diane calls, though the world is crashing down around her. "I'm coming, Mom, I'm coming…"

DIANE WOKE to the sound of distant thunder. *Mom,* she thought groggily. *It's Mom. She's come back for me.* Then she sat up and the dream evaporated like dew drops.

Work. Her presentation. They both came flooding back in a humiliating rush. She wanted to die.

Grow up, Diane.

No, a part of her thought, *I don't want to grow up.* But she pinned that part of herself to the wall and placed it in a headlock. She was *not* a little girl, not anymore. She had to be strong. Whatever was happening to her, she had to be strong.

Mom.

The word hit her heart hard and she started to cry.

Why did you abandon me?

Then came a vision of the tree, standing tall, waiting for her to return to the park.

Madness. Sheer and utter madness. Enraged by emotions that were no longer hers to control, Diane slammed her fists into her pillow. Tears spilled from her eyes, followed by massive, heart-rending sobs.

Grow up, Diane! Get a hold of yourself.

And, superimposed over that first thought, came another from the part of herself she'd imprisoned long ago.

Why, Mom? Why?

She tried to pull herself together—tried to tell herself everything was fine, that she was being a baby, that all she had to do was go back to sleep and that everything would right itself in the morning—but she spent all night lying on her back in the dark, strange thoughts bouncing through her head like pinballs.

Over and over, the phrase that had once been her foster mother's motto screamed in her head, desperate to impose order even as Diane's life crumbled all around her.

Grow up, Diane. Grow up!

8.

IT WAS NOW 9:30 in the morning, and Diane was still in bed, eyes sore, head aching. She'd called into work sick a half hour ago, something she'd never done before today.

The world seemed thin and brittle, as if reaching out too quickly or too carelessly might cause it to shatter, and so she just lay there, sunlight spilling in dribs and drabs through the closed drapes.

Diane felt as if she were in limbo, caught between the pull of two opposing worlds. They each held a part of her, vying for control of the other in a fierce tug of war. How long could she withstand those incredible shearing forces before her soul was torn in two?

The tree's summons had been calling to her throughout the night, weaving in and out of her consciousness so that she was no longer certain what was real and what was not. That voice had been accompanied by a vision impossible to ignore: a tree that was more than a tree, regal limbs sprawling toward the sky, searching for her through the sunrise.

Now Diane tried to ignore it, to steer her mind toward other things. More than once, she recalled her ruined presentation and contemplated ways she could redeem herself and therefore her position at PropelIt. It still hurt to think about work, but at least it gave her something different to consider, something different to anchor her to the only world she'd ever known. But the tree's calling was growing more insistent, and she was finding it increasingly difficult to stay focused.

Grow up, Diane!

She could feel the current of that other world slowly dragging her in, and she was afraid.

The clock on her bedside read 10:00 a.m. when she decided she couldn't stand it any longer. She didn't want to answer the tree's siren call, so Diane told herself she was only taking a walk to clear her head, even though that was something she'd never done before. She told herself to go in a different direction, to stick to city streets, but with eyes only half opened, her feet drove her to the very place she'd tried so hard to ignore, a warm September wind nipping at her neck and shoulders.

The park was quiet and still. No kids in the playground. No adults on the asphalt path winding through the green. The entire world seemed to be holding its breath in anticipation.

Diane could feel a tension in the air, crackling like high-voltage wires. A part of her wanted to look up, find the tree in the distance, and hold its gaze forever. Instead she kept her head down, examining the cracks and deformities in the asphalt, mentally picking apart and rearranging her failed presentation. She had to stay focused on work, had to avoid unearthing that deeper dissatisfaction that had festered for so many years like a gangrenous sore.

But again and again her mind strayed, snagging on the branches of that majestic tree. A certainty was blooming inside of her despite the rational assertions she kept throwing up in self-defense, despite the voice inside that warned her that her mind was cracking around the edges. The tree wasn't a tree at all. The physical form in the park was only a surface reality, a thin shell beneath which something deeper stirred.

Grow up, Diane. A tree's a tree.

All the same, Diane sought its shade like a heat-seeking missile, and once found, she took up residence on the bench beneath its branches, gazing upward, eyes glazed and unfocused. She thought of that campus Christian she'd encountered so many years ago, the kind young man who'd told her that he and his companions were not of this world. The assertion had startled her in a way she hadn't understood at the time, knocking her off balance for the rest of the day. Now she wondered if that was because he'd tapped into something vital, something vulnerable within herself, for Diane was increasingly certain that she, too, was not of this world.

"What do you want from me?" she whispered.

"To take you home, Daughter."

Unexpected and immediate, the tree's answer startled her as much as the young campus Christian's statement had. Though the voice was without sound, the words took root in Diane's mind and blossomed, sending her reeling, craning her head skyward.

It spoke to me. The tree spoke to me.

Diane had been hearing it call for a while, but this was the first time the tree had spoken plainly.

It spoke to me, and it called me Daughter.

Tears sprang to her eyes at the unlikely title, and she stared at the branches and the trunk, unable to speak, refusing to accept the reality of her situation.

Trees don't talk. Grow up, Diane!

And yet…

Diane dropped her head into her hands and cried.

9.

IF DIANE HAD BROUGHT her phone with her, she would have realized it was already 4:30. But she hadn't, and even now, she continued to sit beneath the tree's canopy, staring up at the dappled light shining through the leaves.

She'd remained in the park until lunchtime, then returned home for fear of being spotted by a coworker. Sometime after 1:00, the tree's call had sounded once more, and by 1:45 Diane was back in the park, staring at its branches.

The sun had just started its long descent toward the horizon, and in another hour, people would begin filtering out of the office. She didn't want anyone to see her staring skyward like a loon, but she couldn't move. She was a fly caught in an intricate, otherworldly web and she couldn't look away.

Was this what it felt like to lose one's mind? She realized that crazy people didn't know they were crazy and that if you were lucid enough to question your sanity, you were likely sound of mind. Now, however, she doubted it. The tree's pull had grown so strong. She felt like a piece of iron caught by the pull of a powerful electromagnet. She wanted to fly toward it, to soar through space and time, but she was scared.

Grow up, Diane!

The adult part of her mind was trying so hard to keep her anchored, but she was already sinking and she didn't think she could hold on to herself any longer.

Would it be so bad to go insane? At least crazy people didn't have to worry about whether they belonged; at least crazy people didn't have to worry about fulfilling their life's purpose. Their minds manufactured whatever they needed so they could live their entire lives in blessed, ignorant peace.

The tree was singing now, an earthy resonant rumble that pulsed in time to the longing beats of her withered heart. It rushed through her, desperate to impart new life if only she would choose to accept it.

Once more, Diane peered at this scion of the Earth, only a trunk, bark, branches, and leaves on the surface. Beneath this ordinary veneer, there must be something more. She could feel how the branches and roots extended beyond this world, into some dimension outside space and time—understood that they reached depths surpassing anything she could imagine. She wondered: *Is my world out there somewhere, the world where I belong, the world where I was meant to live?*

Grow up, Diane!

Her mind screamed the words, but they were no longer effective. She'd slipped beyond the event horizon and there was no turning back. Not now, not ever.

The tree paralleled her own interior voice.

"You can grow up, Diane. You can mature into who and what you were destined to be, if only you'll let me take you home."

Diane wanted more than anything to belong, wanted more than anything to manifest her true nature. For so long she'd drowned that desire, trying to snuff it out beneath the unyielding weight of career and responsibility. Those two things had been her drug of choice, helping her to forget the deeper questions that haunted her in the small hours of the night.

But those questions had never died. They were too firmly ingrained in her soul, and she was just beginning to learn that the soul was immortal and could not die, not even in part.

"Come to me, Daughter. Let me take you home."

Yes, she thought dreamily, the old barriers in her mind breaking down at last. *Take me home. Turn me into what I was created to be.*

"All you have to do is take my hand."

Yes, thought Diane, getting up and walking toward the trunk. *All I have to do is take your hand.*

She touched the bark, let her hand explore its rough and gnarled contours. She could feel the familiar power on the inside, surging just beneath the surface, arcing toward her like electricity. A spark jumped from the trunk into her and time froze.

Startled, Diane tried to pull away. But her hand was stuck to the bark. The world dimmed, and before she understood what was happening, she found herself suspended in a place where time and space held no meaning, where she could be or do anything, an endless vista of possibility and potential.

Diane was now alive in a way she'd never been before.

She passed through a barrier, a thin and sticky film, and noted that the world around her was no longer anything like Earth but a universe of abstractions, a spiritual fabric conceived of pure logic and thought. She had senses there, but they were only vaguely analogous to those she'd possessed on Earth.

Diane beheld the whole of that place as if she were gazing down from a tremendous height, her vision filled with the panoramic view of a shimmering alien valley. And before her, at the root of everything, was the tree, not a tree at all in this place but something greater, celestial and divine, a transfiguration of light and energy.

With the sort of knowledge that only came from on high, she understood that the tree ruled over this world and that it had set roots down in thousands of others. This being touched on all living things, ageless and eternal, and Diane could feel the life force of every creature, every universe, flow through its ancient veins, its nature as clear to her as a pane of polished glass. This being before her defied definition. It simply *was*, and she was swept away by the world-shattering assertion of its existence.

Diane staggered back and fell to her knees in silent wonder.

"Welcome home, Daughter."

10.

DAUGHTER.

Once again, this strange being had called her *Daughter*. So-mething stirred in her soul at the use of the word, a part of her truest essence that erupted in a fount of instant recognition and unconstrained joy. But that didn't make sense. There was no way she could be the daughter of such a sprawling, powerful en-tity. She was only human, a pale shade of this being's almighty stature.

"You are so much more than you realize." The words came rushing into her as if the tree had read her mind.

Diane couldn't speak, could only continue kneeling and staring.

"By existing in the human world, you were bound by its laws and forced to take human form. You're free of those constraints now and will realize your potential in time."

The frailty of her human mind had already started to peel away, leaving behind a purer self capable of comprehending this pivotal truth.

You're my mother.

"Yes, Daughter."

Something like sorrow rippled through her, a terrible aching bewilderment. It was not an emotion. Emotions were things her human mind had manufactured in the human world. What she felt here was somehow richer, fuller. If her body had been there with her, tears would have streamed down the sides of her face and she would have rent her garments in agony.

Her mother. As incredible as it was to believe, this being that stood before her was her *mother.*

Why did you abandon me?

"I would never abandon you. I love you."

Sorrow gave way to a flash flood of rage.

You left me in front of a library in a cardboard box. I was only a baby.

Sadness and grief. Both feelings, though they belonged to the tree, passed through Diane as if they were her own, as if the two of them were connected by some hidden umbilicus.

I was raised by foster parents who didn't love me. My childhood was a mystery. I've spent my whole life wondering who I am and who you were.

"I had no choice. Our world was under attack. I couldn't risk losing you, so I sent you away."

And in that moment, a vision overcame her.

THE CAELEST, once a noble race but now a horde of darkness, descend over the cosmos like an Old Testament plague, consuming everything in their path and leaving nothing but blight and ruin in their wake. Diane, who is no longer Diane but her mother, the Queen, gazes upon the senseless destruction of her realm, helpless, rivers of sorrow flowing down her regal cheeks.

She tries to fend them off, has even fared well in battle until now, but she knew before the fighting began that they would overpower her defenses, just as they had broken through so many others. Once, eons ago, she engaged them and won, securing a special place for herself among the stars. Now they've returned, and this time they have the advantage.

The worlds under her stewardship are dying. She glances back at the daughter by her side, her rightful heir, the manifestation of a love so strong it took on a life of its own. This place isn't safe for her anymore. She must be sent away, to a far-off world that doesn't yet know the full extent of the blight.

A profound despair grips her as she considers the prospect of leaving her offspring alone in a world so inhospitable to her kind. She wants to go with her daughter, but she knows she can't. She must stay behind to defend her realm.

So the Queen sends her daughter away.

In the terrible agony that follows there is endless black, all consuming, ever reaching, everlasting. The Caelest sweep through her realm, taking her into themselves, feeding off her essence. She fights, pitting her dimmed light against their deepening dark in a never-ending struggle of despair. Their darkness overcame long ago, yet still she holds. She is the cornerstone, the foundation upon which everything else is built, and they cannot destroy her realm until they've vanquished her.

Then light, blinding. The Immortals, sweeping through her universe. They filter, refine, cleanse. She bursts with joy when at last she emerges from the darkness unscathed. Her struggle, she is overjoyed to learn, was not in vain.

But her heart aches.

Daughter.

She reaches out across space and time, hoping it isn't too late, that Earth's constricting laws haven't bound her daughter so tightly that she's lost her true nature. And at last, after eons of searching her expansive network of celestial roots, she makes contact. She sees that Diane, though wounded, remains whole. So she calls, and she waits, and after a time, her daughter answers…

DIANE SHOOK HER HEAD, casting off the vision like a nightmare. It was too much too fast. Her mind was short-circuiting, refusing to acknowledge the truth.

She needed space. She needed time to think.

I have to go.

"Please, Daughter. Don't leave. You were made for so much more."

Anguish, heart-wrenching. The tree's feelings of loss and regret poured into her like an ocean.

All her life, Diane had imagined what her mother was like, had wondered why she'd abandoned her. Now, here at last was the woman she'd wanted to confront, and she discovered that knowing the truth was more painful. Somehow, it made the loss more real rather than less.

I have to go, Diane repeats. *I have work, responsibilities.*

Diane could feel the tree wither inside, an aching despair that was mirrored in her. But she was also angry at her mother for sending her away, angry that the meager life she'd built around herself had come crashing down without warning.

Finally, the tree sighed, a mournful breeze that swept through the entirety of her realm.

"As you wish."

Overcome with emotion, Diane closed her eyes. She felt herself pass back through that sticky barrier between worlds, and for a moment she wanted to cry out, to tell her mother she'd made a mistake and that she wanted to stay after all. Then it was over, and she was opening her eyes once more to the park, surrounded by green, now dimmed by the impending shadows of twilight. Earth had become bland to her, mute and pale, and Diane couldn't help but feel she'd lost something essential.

She gazed at the tree, but it no longer spoke to her. It was only a tree, silent and still, its branches slightly drooped. She sensed a lingering sadness and regret, but it was just an afterimage, burned into the retinas of her soul.

Diane shivered, and it was long after dark when she finally stumbled home to her apartment, defeated and broken.

11.

DIANE WANDERED THE PARK the following day, staring at the sky as if trapped in a dream from which she couldn't wake. It was late morning, well past when she should have gone to work. She hadn't bothered to call.

Wearing shorts and a T-shirt instead of her usual dress shirt and skirt, she ambled across the grass like a ship with a broken sail, adrift, splintered, and searching for something that would be forever out of reach. It was eerily quiet, with not even the cawing of a crow to break the pall of silence that had settled over the world.

Her gaze swept over the park's periphery, and an atavistic shock ran through her when her eyes locked on the tree, rising up from the earth ahead. Its branches had taken on a skeletal appearance, and the leaves had started to turn yellow where only a day ago they'd been a vibrant green.

Diane's stomach clenched, and for a moment she thought she'd be sick.

Mother.

She half expected her mind to throw out its usual mantra in reply: *Grow up, Diane!* But that voice was dead now. She'd transformed into the little girl she'd tried so hard to suppress, the little girl she'd never allowed herself to be growing up, and now she was lost, surrounded by things she didn't understand in a hostile alien world.

She paused, perhaps hoping for the tree to reply. But when it was clear that silence would be her only answer, she cast her eyes down and passed it by, working her way instead toward the office.

As Diane walked, she replayed yesterday's encounter with her mother in her head. She asked herself if she'd done the right thing, if she shouldn't instead have stayed in that other world. But the wound was still so fresh, so raw, that she couldn't think straight. Her mind was a jumble of contradictory thoughts, emotions, and desires, and she honestly had no idea what she wanted.

There was still a fevered voice inside that insisted she return to work, that she should salvage whatever tatters remained of her career before she ended up on the streets. As if in reply, Diane's office came into view, jutting out before her, its drab geometric walls reminding her more of a prison than a place of work. Was this what she'd always been so eager to belong to? She made a wide arc around the building's perimeter, not wanting to encounter any of her coworkers.

Ex-coworkers.

The thought sprung to life against her will, and the part of her that still believed she could go back to the way things were reeled at the inevitable, irrevocable truth: she'd severed her last remaining tie to the Earth, and now there was nothing left for her. Diane wanted to cry, but no tears would come, only a numb ache that was somehow so much worse.

The park was pale like the leaves on the tree, desiccated and dying, and she couldn't stand to be there any longer. It was too painful, a constant reminder of what she'd briefly had and let slip through her fingers. So she turned around, still avoiding the tree that would no longer speak to her, and returned to her apartment with her head down.

12.

DIANE SPENT THE NEXT WEEK and a half barricaded indoors. She'd thrown her phone out the three-story window and was no longer answering emails. At one point, someone had knocked on the door, but when she didn't answer they left her alone. Coworkers checking in on her? Didn't know, didn't matter. Her old life was over now. There was no way she could go back. She'd never felt like she belonged before, but now she knew the awful truth: that this world had never been home to begin with. She couldn't help feeling like she had nowhere left to go, that she was now little more than a cosmic vagrant, drifting through time and space without a place to hang her hat and call her own.

One afternoon, Diane lay in bed with the covers up to her waist, turned toward the window to gaze upon the city beneath. It spread before her like the picked-over, sun-bleached bones of a prehistoric animal, barren, lifeless, and dry.

A part of her wanted to jump out of bed, to go running back

into her mother's arms. But she wasn't ready to do that yet, and at any rate, she didn't even know if it was possible. Diane hadn't heard the tree's voice since she'd returned from that other world, and she feared she never would again.

I've made an awful mistake.

Then she thought of the sterile, loveless environment she'd grown up in because her mother had left her here alone, and once more the heat of her anger sliced through her chest like a knife. The one who should have loved her above all else had instead sent her away at her most vulnerable.

On and on her thoughts went, circling back and forth, oscillating between anger and despair, until she tired herself out and fell asleep.

Diane got up once around 3:00 p.m. to eat a sandwich because her stomach had knotted with hunger. But the food tasted like ash and she had a hard time swallowing. When she finished eating, she chased it down with a glass of lukewarm water. She returned to bed soon after without brushing her teeth, and she didn't stir again until the following morning.

13.

TIME STARTED to run together. Diane hardly ate or drank except when the pain in her stomach became too difficult to ignore. She would slip back and forth between sleep and consciousness, lost in the hopeless no-man's-land between, until she had trouble differentiating between the two states. Sometimes, Diane swore she could still hear the tree. A longing would swell inside her heart and she would think it wasn't too late after all, that she still had time to change her mind. Then she'd come back to herself and there would only be the dim silence of her shuttered apartment. Just a dream, she would think, and she would slip back into the twilight of semi-consciousness. Like fruit too long off the vine, her heart had already started to shrivel and dry.

Diane used to fear pain as a child. Only now did she realize she'd been afraid of the wrong thing. The opposite of contentment was not anguish and suffering but the cold, emotionless void of despair. She couldn't go on like this. She had to do something, whatever it took to make her feel again. Her old life was over, and she couldn't go back to the tree. There was only one thing left to do.

Lightheaded and weak, Diane pulled herself out of bed. She fixed a sandwich made of leftover ham and washed it down with water. She showered, changed into a T-shirt, jeans, and a coat. Fishing through her closet, she found a faded canvas bag she hadn't carried since college. She filled it with two days' worth of clothes, then added her wallet and keys.

Finally, slinging the bag over her shoulder, she looked back one last time at her bedroom—at the work papers strewn across the floor and the desk, at the nightstand where she'd kept her laptop before abandoning it at the office. All worthless trinkets now, relics of a former life.

Diane stepped outside, squinted up at the burning light of the sun, and started toward the street. She didn't bother closing the door behind her.

14.

THE BUS DOORS OPENED, and Diane stepped off into the Greyhound parking lot. She turned her face toward the bright early-afternoon sun, but in Alamogordo, New Mexico, in the middle of December, it offered little warmth. Diane shivered, breath pluming in the air like smoke, and adjusted the wool beanie she'd bought in Lordsburg. With a sigh, she made her way past the squat blue bus station toward a narrow two-lane highway.

Diane's exodus had so far lasted two and a half months, with stops in Arizona and New Mexico. She had no particular destination in mind. She knew only that she had to keep moving. The thing she needed to feel whole was out there somewhere and she would wander through the desert for forty years if that was what it took to find it.

The small historic city was dusty, old, and looked as if it belonged in a movie straight out of the 1960s. A more innocent time, Diane thought. She hadn't been alive in the '60s, but she'd seen a lot of films growing up, like *Mary Poppins*, *Chitty Chitty Bang Bang*, and *The Parent Trap*, all vibrant psychedelic colors and passionate, delirious optimism. But like the world in which those films were born, the colors had faded, leaving behind only washed-out memories and hopeless reminders of all that had been lost in the intervening decades.

Near the bus station, Diane spotted a cheap two-story motel called The Satellite Inn. It looked as good a place as any to spend the night. She peered up at the sign, a sleek space-age model of the atom, and stepped inside.

"Can I help you?" asked a man at the front desk. Lloyd, according to the name tag on his shirt.

"I need a room."

Lloyd looked like he'd rather be anyplace else. Maybe he had a family to go home to when his shift was over. Diane's eyes suddenly stung, and she froze mid-stride as if she'd been slapped.

"You all right?" All at once, the weariness drained out of Lloyd's eyes.

He was concerned for her, she realized. It was the same look some of her coworkers had given her the day of the presentation.

There are people who care.

Her mother had cared, too. Not her foster mother, but her *true* mother, the tree…

No, can't think about that.

"Fine," she said, shaking herself. "I'm fine."

And then Diane lost it. Desperate, hitching sobs burst out of her like angry demons, twisting her insides, turning her nose into an avalanche of snot. Lloyd was by her side in a heartbeat, helping her find a chair, handing her a tissue, asking again if she was okay, if she needed help.

"No," said Diane, chest heaving. "No, thank you. I just need— I just want to rest." She punctuated this with a long honking blast into her tissue.

"You need anything? Some water?"

Gazing into his eyes, she almost lost it again.

"No, Lloyd. Really, I'm fine. Just give me a room."

"All right," he said, returning to his station behind the counter. "A room, sure. We've got plenty of vacancies. Just a moment."

What had gotten into her? He must think she was insane. She had to be strong. The tree, as well as her job and the coworkers she'd left behind, was a part of her old life, and it was time to move on.

"Room 215," said Lloyd, "On the second floor. Queen bed, only forty-five dollars."

"That sounds lovely." Having gotten her breathing under control, Diane got up, reached into her bag, and handed him her credit card. She hadn't made a payment since her exodus from Irvine, but they hadn't yet closed her account and she might as well ride that train while it lasted. What was the worst that could happen? She'd trash her credit score? The debt would go into collections? Good luck to anyone who tried to track her down. The last address her bank had on file was an abandoned apartment that, for all she knew, had been rented out already.

Visibly relieved, Lloyd processed her payment, then handed her a key card along with a piece of paper with a code to access the Wi-Fi.

"Check out's at twelve," he said, eying her, "but if you need a little extra time…"

"I understand. Thank you."

Really, what had gotten into her, Diane thought as she picked her way up a series of chipped concrete stairs. She could do this. She was strong. She could find her own way.

The light in Diane's room was dim when she opened the door and turned it on, but that suited her just fine. All she wanted to do was sleep.

15.

"DIANE."

She opened her mouth to speak—*I'm here*, she wanted to say—but it was as if someone else were fighting for control of her body. She could feel the muscles in her face tense as she tried to form a reply, but there was another will inside of her, another Diane, dead set on ignoring her mother's anguished call.

"Diane, please, come back to me."

I'm here, she tried to say again, but Other Diane wasn't having any of that.

—That part of your life is over now. Move on.

No, she thought. *No, I need her.*

—You made your choice, now live with it.

No! The world blurred around her as she tussled with herself, flashes of ethereal colors and lights streaking past her in a frenzied blur. Diane had to get back to where she belonged, had to return to the only being who'd ever loved her. But Other Diane was always right in front of her, blocking her way.

"Daughter, please."

The muscles in her neck had bunched into thick corded knots. *Let me speak to her*, she tried to say, but Other Diane only threw her head back and roared with bitter laughter.

—You should have gone when you had the chance.

She's calling to me, thought Diane, *can't you see that? It's not too late!*

—Move on.

I want to go.

—Move on!

The battle raged on, a struggle of tectonic proportions. All the while, her mother called to her from some unfathomable distance.

"Diane."

"Diane."

"Diane…"

DIANE SURGED into consciousness, screaming.

"I'm here! Mother, I'm here!" But she had only the darkness of her motel room for a reply. This was not the same room she'd rented six months ago at The Satellite Inn, but a dingy fleabag single at a no-name motel outside the Vegas Strip. She groped for the lamp on the nightstand, remembered the electricity wasn't working, shot out of bed, and stepped into the night.

The moon was full, bathing the balcony in a pallid monochromatic light. Diane grabbed the railing, hands trembling, and looked down at the parking lot below.

The dreams had started a few weeks ago, shortly after her credit card was declined. She'd had to resort to pulling cash out of an ATM, and she was doing her best to stretch what little she had left. Three months. She could manage for three months if she scrimped and saved. And then? Diane preferred not to think about that.

Just stress dreams, she thought. She was worried about money, worried about food and shelter. But she knew there was more to it than that.

Maybe it's not too late. A tiny ray of hope pierced her private darkness like a spear. *Maybe I can still go back.* But she was reprimanded at once by an angry, self-reviling thought.

Bullshit. You made your choice, now live with it.

The thought was right. She'd made her choice, and it was too late to go back. She would have to find her own way.

But she could—

No choice.

Almost shaking with cold though it was over a hundred and ten degrees, Diane slipped back into her room and closed the door.

16.

DIANE WOKE to the sound of a honking semi. Her eyes fluttered open, then squinted shut against a bright and painful light. Had she left the lamp on in her motel? No, her last stay in a motel had been a couple of weeks ago. She became aware of a pain in the small of her back, a dull and throbbing ache. Coming fully awake now, she bolted upright.

The adobe bench beneath her was hard and unyielding. Diane couldn't believe she'd spent the night on it. What she'd mistaken for a bedside lamp was the sun, filtering down through a copse of trees in a park in Laughlin, Nevada.

As she now did most mornings after waking, Diane wondered how she could have fallen so far and how things could have gotten so bad.

The grass around her was a vibrant green, an oasis of suburbia in the middle of an otherwise dry and barren desert. The playground was empty—it was still early, and it was a weekday, so the kids would be at school—but she thought she'd better get a move on if she didn't want to spend the afternoon in the back of a policeman's car.

Diane adjusted the beanie on her head, the same one she'd bought in New Mexico, now tattered, faded, and torn. It was mid-October, and though it wasn't yet the freezing cold of winter, the weather was already beginning to cool. She stared up at the leaves of the trees and a deep, mournful ague rippled through her. She tried her best not to think about what she'd lost a little more than a year ago.

Diane got to her feet and continued on.

When her money started running thin, Diane had resorted to sleeping on park benches and at bus stops. All her life, she'd slept on comfortable mattresses and couches—about the worst she'd experienced was a night on the floor of her office after working late—and she hadn't been prepared for the toughness of the streets. She hadn't even thought to secure her bag during her first tentless camping trip, a mistake she sorely regretted when she awoke the following morning to find her meager belongings and tattered wallet stolen.

Diane had wanted to cry out to her mother, to beg her to take her back. But there was still something inside of her that believed she could find her own way.

You can't go back. It's too late. You made your bed, now lie in it.

So she clung to this terrible half-life and continued to drift from one place to the next, her travels confined to Nevada now that she could no longer afford public transportation.

There was actually a perverse sort of attraction in her new life, a dawning awareness that she could slip through the cracks of the world unseen. She'd gone rogue and was now a citizen of the underworld. She could do whatever she wanted as long as she didn't brush against the wrong side of the law. There would be nobody to rebuke her, nobody to tell her she'd done a bad job or that she hadn't worked hard enough. It wasn't much consolation, but optimism was in short supply and Diane would hang on to whatever she could find.

Her stomach rumbled, and for a moment old habits got the best of her. She reached for her shoulder where her bag had once hung, then felt along the lining of her shorts pockets before remembering her wallet was gone. She wouldn't beg. She didn't have much pride left, but that, at least, remained beneath her. Nor would she set out in search of a trash can or a dumpster. The very notion made her sick, and she didn't think she'd go quite that far unless her ribs started poking through her skin. No, she would do the same thing she'd been doing since she first found herself on the streets.

Diane set off for the city in search of an outdoor restaurant, hands trembling like a drug addict's, and once again wondered how she could have sunk so low so fast.

17.

THE TRICK, thought Diane, sitting at an outdoor table in front of an In-N-Out Burger, was to sit and wait for someone with food to use the bathroom, or to get a refill on their drink, or to talk to the cashier, then to slip quietly past their table and snatch whatever was left. There weren't many who left their food unattended, but if she waited long enough, she'd always find someone.

Of course, she never frequented the same restaurant twice. There were CCTVs, and if enough customers complained, it wouldn't be long before she was caught. Diane had always prided herself on being a careful woman.

Whenever she thought about how good she was getting at stealing other people's food, a pang of guilt rippled through her.

But they can afford to pay for another meal. It's just a minor inconvenience for them.

She tried not to think about how angry she would have been if someone had stolen her own meal.

Diane watched and waited, stomach growling in heated protest as the hour slipped from nine to ten, then from ten to eleven. She was considering visiting the restroom when a young guy in his late teens ducked inside, leaving behind a Double-Double with fries.

Diane's mouth watered and she leaped to her feet, preparing to grab it. She strolled across the concrete dining area, pretending to look for a more comfortable place to sit, then caught sight of her reflection in a nearby window and froze.

The woman staring back at her was not Diane at all but a stranger, feral and ungroomed, with dirt smeared across her face and shoulders. An aboriginal from deep within the heart of an urban jungle. She shook her head as if doing so might dispel this awful vision, as if her refusal to acknowledge what she'd become had the power to absolve her of her past and set her upon the proper path once more.

But the reflection remained unchanged and Diane could only stare with mute horror.

This isn't who I am.

And to her surprise, the self-reviling voice that had been so active these past few weeks had nothing left to say.

What have I become?

This wasn't who Diane was supposed to be. Who was she kidding? She'd spent all this time on the open road searching for a place to belong, but the truth was that without her mother, she would never find a place to belong because Earth wasn't her home. There was only one entity out there in all the cosmos that could rescue her, and Diane called out to her now.

Mother?

No reply at all except for the glimmer of hope that passed across her features in the window's reflection, like a flash of sunlight from behind a moving cloud. A breeze kicked up behind her, a dusty October sigh that made her skin prickle. Diane's breath caught in her throat. There was so much she needed to say, and she didn't know where to begin.

I'm sorry, Mother. I shouldn't have left. I was angry and confused. Everything changed so fast and I wasn't prepared. I need you. Please, take me back.

"*I never left you, Daughter.*"

Diane staggered, unaware that the people around her were starting to stare. The tree had finally spoken.

The walls of a colossal dam burst inside her head and a tidal wave of emotion nearly knocked her to the ground.

"*Please, come home.*"

Diane erupted in a maelstrom of tears and snot. Her mother had never abandoned her. She'd only given Diane the space she needed to finally let go of whatever still tied her to the Earth. Now that she was free, now that she was ready, her mother would embrace her and put an end to her long exile.

"Are you okay?"

Startled, Diane turned. A man in a suit and tie gazed down at her, not with a look of disgust, as so many others had given her, but with one of genuine concern.

"I'm fine," she said, and she sobbed even harder.

"Can I get you something? Are you hungry?"

"No," said Diane, her appetite forgotten. "No need. I just realized I'm not where I belong and that it's time for me to go home."

He stared at her, dumbstruck, and Diane could only laugh.

"Thank you," she said while he continued to stand there, head cocked and mouth agape. "I'm okay, but thank you."

With those final words, Diane bounded across the street in search of a destiny that, at long last, would be fulfilled.

18.

THE JOURNEY HOME was long and arduous. Without money or a car, Diane was forced to beg for change that she could use to ride the bus, or else stand by the roadside with her thumb cocked west, hoping whoever picked her up wouldn't murder her or turn her into a human trafficking statistic. Faced with such adversity, Diane concluded that she'd truly hit rock bottom.

There was a time when such a realization would have destroyed her. Now, however, she was discovering that there was freedom in surrender. She used to believe that you had to put in the never-ending work to cultivate the life you wanted. But in the intervening months, she'd learned that there was no such thing as control, only the illusion of it. It was like a mirage in a hot and sprawling desert, always within eyeshot but never within reach.

You could spend your entire life doing everything by the book, preparing for the perfect career, the perfect marriage, the perfect family, only for life to bludgeon you over the head one day and take it all away. The only real sort of control was how you responded to your current circumstances, and now, instead of refusing to acknowledge reality, Diane had decided to face it. Instead of plowing ahead with her preconceived notions of how life should have turned out and running away with her tail between her legs when it all went wrong, Diane would accept life on its own terms.

She was standing at the corner of Beach Blvd. and Orangethorpe Ave. at a little past five in the morning—the final leg of her journey, she hoped, while praying to her mother for protection—when a woman pulled up at a red light and rolled down her window.

"Where you headed?" she asked.

"Irvine." And then Diane added, with only a touch of desperation, "I'm trying to get home."

Her heart leaped into her throat as she waited for a response. She'd been standing on this same street corner since last night and had faced one rejection after another—and given her appearance and the inherently dangerous nature of picking up hitchhikers, was that really so surprising? But Diane wasn't sure she could take another disappointment.

The woman looked her up and down. She hesitated, but after a silent interior battle, shown only in a rapid procession of shifting facial expressions, the woman at last nodded and said,

"Hop in."

Diane's heart swelled and she struggled to hold back tears.

"Thank you," she half whispered, voice hoarser than she would have cared to admit. "Thank you so much."

Diane heard her mother then: *"See you soon, Daughter."* She wasn't sure if it was real or only in her head, but either way she held it close to her heart.

See you soon, Mother.

19.

FIRST, THEY HOPPED onto the 91 East. Then they merged onto the 5 South. Even at five in the morning, cars were piling up, and by the time they started through Santa Ana, traffic was already bumper to bumper. Despite all that had happened, Diane remained self-conscious. Passing encounters with strangers were one thing; sharing a car with one was quite another.

The woman had asked her a few questions, and Diane had answered them graciously, but as soon as the questions stopped, Diane directed her eyes out the window and didn't look back. She watched people sail across her field of vision, all contributing to the morning rush she herself had been a part of not too long ago. In a different life.

Looking back at her former self was like looking through the wrong end of a telescope. It all felt so distant and strange, as if past Diane had been someone else entirely. How could that career-driven individual ever have learned to see beyond the four walls of her office? She'd undergone such a radical transformation in such a short period, and she could only marvel at how completely and efficiently her mother had upended her world.

But she'd done it out of love.

It was only because of Diane's stubborn attachment to this pallid life on Earth that she hadn't been able to go to her mother that very same day in the park. She'd needed time to think, to process the startling revelation. But once she was ready, her mother had been there, waiting.

Diane wondered how long the tree had been calling to her. Had it started that distant day in the park or had it been earlier? She thought of the many restless years she'd spent earning her degree and then toiling through one job after the next, the phrase she'd learned from a campus Christian never far from her mind: *Not of this world.* She thought of the many circumstances that had led her to accept that final job in Irvine, which turned out to be just a means of discovering the park and the mystical tree at its center. She reflected on all this during the mostly standstill ride through Santa Ana and decided, upon due consideration, that there was no such thing as coincidence. Her mother, in one form or another, must have always been looking out for her, planting seeds at regular intervals throughout her life that would eventually lead Diane home.

"You look like you've had a rough couple of days."

"What?" Diane had been staring out the window and was

caught off guard by the statement.

"I don't mean to pry. I just thought— If you're in trouble, if you need anything—" The woman's eyes never strayed from the road ahead.

"Thank you," said Diane, looking down and folding her hands in her lap, "but you've done more than enough for me already."

They'd just exited Santa Ana and were trying to merge onto the 55. Diane watched the road curve to the right, her heart somersaulting in her chest. She was beginning to feel her mother's pull, a slight tugging on her heart.

I'm close now.

Like a bride-to-be, Diane discovered she was nervous. Today was her last day in the human world. After that... Well, after that, her life would change.

"Are you sure? Again, I don't mean to pry, but if you're hungry, if you need some fresh clothes..."

"I just want to go home, but thank you."

The woman nodded. "If you change your mind—"

"I'll let you know." Then, after a brief pause, "I hope I didn't take you too far out of your way."

The woman shrugged. "I work in the area. No big deal."

Diane turned, and for the first time since getting into the car, she got a good look at her gracious benefactor. Dressed in a dark gray pencil skirt and matching V-neck top, it was clear to Diane that she worked in an office, and judging by the thick leather portfolio resting beside her, the woman must have been an important member of the team. Maybe an executive, or even an officer. It felt so much like staring at her former self that she almost recoiled in shock.

This could easily have been me.

Only this woman was kinder and more charitable than Diane had been. If their roles had been reversed, if she'd seen herself on the roadside clothed in soiled rags, she never would have paid her even a moment's notice, let alone stopped.

"Thank you," Diane said again. "You don't know how much this ride means to me. The last few months have been difficult. I wish there was something I could do to make it up to you."

"When I was down on my luck, a stranger helped me, too. I finished school and landed the job I have today, all because of her, all because she took a chance on me. I don't know where I'd be today without her help, and I just wanted to pay it forward, you know?"

Diane nodded, unable to think of a suitable reply. Instead, tears brimmed at the corners of her eyes. This was how the world should be. Through this woman's selfless act, she could feel her mother's love shining forth like a beacon.

That, thought Diane, was the true purpose of life: to love and to be loved, a purpose that would no doubt bring this woman happiness throughout her years, and that would sustain

Diane in the life to come.

"That's my exit," said Diane, and when the woman finally pulled off the freeway onto Culver Drive and headed toward the park, tears of joy spasmed out of her.

"Are you all right?" the woman asked, turning at last, and Diane thought of the man in Nevada who'd asked her much the same question.

"I'm fine," she said. "It just feels so good to come home."

20.

"ARE YOU SURE you want me to let you out here?"

The woman had pulled up within viewing distance of the park, and Diane was eager to hop out. But she didn't want to be rude, not when this woman had shown her so much kindness.

"Yes," Diane said. "The apartment I'm looking for is just across the park."

"I could drop you a little closer."

"No, this is perfect. I like to walk."

"All right, if you're sure." Though the woman obviously was not.

"Listen, I just want to say…thank you again, for everything."

The woman shrugged. "It was my pleasure."

And what was that sparkle Diane thought she spied in the woman's eyes? Surely not tears. A lengthy pause passed between the two of them, and Diane was just about to let herself out when the woman spoke again.

"Actually, if you want the God's honest truth, when I saw

you standing there on the street corner, I wasn't sure I should let you in. You know, stranger danger and all of that. But then I saw something in the way you looked at me, and I thought, I don't know, maybe there was a reason I was there. Maybe I was supposed to pick you up. Does that sound crazy?"

Once more, Diane thought about her long journey through life and concluded that there was no such thing as coincidence.

"No," she said. "No, it doesn't sound crazy at all."

"It felt like providence, or fate, or whatever you want to call it. Hell, I don't know if I believe in God, but I'm certain now that I was meant to be there. I just hope… I hope that whatever it is you need, wherever it is you're going, you get there safely and find what you're looking for."

"Don't worry, I already have."

The woman offered her hand and Diane shook it.

"Good luck," said the woman.

Diane stepped out of the car at last. She inhaled the biting early November air and felt alive for the first time in months. On impulse, she turned back—just in time, it turned out, to catch the woman mid-wave. Diane waved back, and after the woman had pulled back into traffic, she stood there on the threshold of her new life, trembling with anticipation.

This is it. No turning back now.

The air around her seemed to quiver with the weight of her mother's promise, and Diane, caught up in its sweeping embrace, would keep her waiting no longer.

85

21.

THE SUN HAD JUST CRESTED the horizon, tinting the whole world gold, when Diane broke into a fevered sprint. She was malnourished and deconditioned, and it wasn't long before the growing stitch in her side became a lance piercing deep into her flesh. But she kept running, kept pressing forward. Pain was a distant thing, a human trifle soon to be of little concern.

Diane closed the space between herself and the park in a matter of seconds, and when she stepped off the street and onto the grass, a delirious thrill shot through her.

"Daughter."

Her mother's voice was unmistakable now. It filled the hollow spaces around her, infusing the environment with extra-dimensional substance and form. Like a powerful radio signal, that voice had been broadcast into the world, and now that Diane had closed in on its source, she could feel it rippling through her, touching that part of herself she'd tried and failed for so many years to silence.

Bright rays of early-morning sunlight pierced the canopy of trees, lending the park an otherworldly glow, and at its center, where the light was brightest, was the tree—*My mother*—no longer sickly and drooping but healthy and erect, a vivid green crowned with gold, sporting roots that extended deep into the earth and beyond.

Savoring the crisp and frigid air that whistled through her ears, Diane sailed along the path like a silver bullet. At last, her exodus from the world where she belonged was over.

The tree grew closer and the light intensified, until finally, Diane was standing beneath the leaves, swaying to the beat of a silent, ancient song. A breeze whistled behind her, giving her goosebumps. And was that just the wind she heard, or something more, something *other*?

Diane's breath caught in her throat and she opened her mouth to speak. But there was so much she needed to say and she didn't know where to begin. Instead she stood there, mouth agape, while the world spun on, indifferent to her impending transformation.

Here she was, home at last. After all she'd been through—the breakdown, the homelessness, and finally her great awakening—a part of herself still expected to hear that all-too-familiar voice of contempt: *Grow up, Diane.* But in her heart, Diane heard only silence, a silence so profound, so complete, it brought tears to her eyes.

"Hello, Mother."

She reached out with unsteady hands, and when they brushed against the coarse bark of the tree, the ageless lifeblood of creation filled her as it had that day in the park long ago. A spark passed between herself and the tree, and a moment later, her heart burst into the blazing flames of a love so massive it was impossible to contain.

Sobs tore through her like a tropical rainstorm, and she welcomed each and every one of them. They were not something to be ashamed of; if anything, they were harbingers of her inner child's release and were something to be celebrated.

Diane knew in that moment that words were useless. There was nothing she could say to express the utmost desire of her heart, nor was there anything that needed to be said.

I'm ready, those silent feelings communicated. *Take me home.*

And just like that, Diane passed through that thin barrier, back into a world she once thought she'd never see again. *Our kingdom is not of this world*, the campus Christian had said so many years ago, and in her case, at least, that belief had proved to be true.

When Diane crossed over—when the old world fell away as it had fallen away once before—she again beheld her mother transfigured and dropped to her knees in reverence.

"Welcome."

Diane looked up to meet her mother's gaze, and she knew,

in that moment, that she was home and that she would never feel out of place again.

Other Books by Jeff Coleman

Dying Breath, a short story (e-book)

Rite of Passage, a short story (e-book and hardcover)

Snapshots: The Collected Flash Fiction of Jeff Coleman, Volume 1 (paperback and hardcover)

The Others, a middle grade fantasy (e-book)

The Sign, a short story (e-book)

The Stronger Half, a novel (e-book, paperback, and hardcover)

Inkbound, a novella (e-book, paperback, and hardcover)

Keep up-to-date with Jeff's latest work by following his blog:

https://blog.jeffcolemanwrites.com/

About the Author

Jeff Coleman's passion for storytelling goes all the way back to third grade, when he wrote his first (not very good) short story about a leprechaun who enjoys eating green food. While growing up, he was captivated by classic Nintendo games like *Zelda*, and later computer games like *Myst*, each of which took place in worlds very unlike our own, and set his imagination aflame with possibilities for his own tales.

During his college years, Jeff fell in love with math, physics and philosophy, subjects that seeded his heart with a profound interest in the many extraordinary mysteries to be found in apparently ordinary things. Jeff is a firm believer that there is more to the universe than immediate appearances suggest, that there is more to our existence than meets the eye. He's therefore fascinated by stories which probe beyond surface observations, stories which attempt to explore the strange and preternatural, stories which unsettle us, which make us think, which make us question what we are and why we're here.

Some of his favorite books are *The Dark Tower*, by Stephen King; *Neverwhere* and *The Ocean at the End of the Lane*, by Neil Gaiman; *The Night Circus*, by Erin Morgenstern; *The Golem and the Jinni*, by Helene Wecker; and *Harry Potter*, by J.K. Rowling.